My Own Colorful Bag Of Stories

A collection of short stories and proses

Swaranya Gupta

Dedication

To my mother who has kept me before all and loved me unconditionally no matter what .....

Contents

Foreword

The first poem that I wrote was at the age of 11, in my classroom, when my english teacher gave me a task to write a poem on the theme of 'Christmas'. At first, I was confused and nervous. Neither had I written a poem before nor did I know how to write one. So, I sat for a while, thinking. I thought about my parents and how they so naturally wrote wonderful poems. This gave me inspiration. I was their daughter, so, if they could write poems then so can I.Soon after, I got an idea. I decided I would write a poem in which the first alphabets of each line would spell out 'Christmas'. At that time I didn't know that this type of a poem was called an Acrostic Poem. Anyways, I wrote the poem and named it, 'A Christmas Eve's Night'. After reading it to myself a few times, I went to my english teacher and handed her the paper I wrote the poem on. She read the poem, looked at me, smiled and again read it. She then told the entire class to stop what they were doing and stand up. Then, she blessed me and quietly said, "Dear, you deserve this and more." She also made me read my poem aloud and the entire class applauded for me.

The years rolled by, and so much has changed all around the world with the coming of COVID-19 and many other issues. Although, the one thing that did not change, even during this period, is my interest and passion in reading and writing stories and poems.

In this collection, I have tried to recreate my feelings during some experiences in life. I hope you will like and enjoy reading them.

I want to thank my mother, Arpita Gupta, for all my achievements, including this book, till date. Had she not insisted, the poems would have remained in my mind for ever.

Kolkata

February 2023

Swaranya Gupta

Looking At Fairy Tales Through The Lens Of Reality

Fairy Tales.....

They say how Cinderella was weak and made no protests.

They say how Ariel foolishly lost her voice for a prince she fell in love with.

They say how Aurora and Snow White were woken after being given a kiss which saved them.

They say how these princesses were frail and fragile, innocent and naive, and, how they were rescued by their Prince Charmings and White Knights in shining armours.

But.....

Did anyone ever tell how Cinderella's step-family very mysteriously vanished from the face of Earth?

How Ariel killed the Prince for betraying her?

How Aurora screamed bloody murder when
woken up to a kiss given by a stranger?
Or, how Snow White went back to the castle
for sweet revenge?

The answer to these questions is beyond a
doubt, **NO!**

They are afraid, afraid to tell us about the
power these legendary women possessed.
That they were not sobbing, feeble maidens
but were powerful and mighty warrior
women.

Women.....

Women, in my dictionary, are defined not
just as grown up females or damsels waiting
for their soul mates to come to their aid.
Neither are they perfectly perfect or
absolutely flawless.

Women, in my dictionary, are warrior
Queens, strength for their loved ones and
admired by them, and, feared by those who
dare to harm the people close to the sacred
place that is their heart.
Women are the ones who are not fearful of
taking destiny in their own hands and
changing history.

Women, real women, are perfectly
imperfect and have real flaws to deal with.

Last but not the least, women are the
females who fight for their rights, for their
freedom, for what is, and was, always theirs.

Dark Days

BAM!

"You all are going to die", he says with smirk.

BAM!

Pain. Screams. Darkness.

"NO!" I woke up with a scream.

"Samantha?"

I snapped my head up, sighing softly as my best friend sauntered over, taking a seat on the stool beside me. I exhaled once more, rubbing a hand over my face. "Hey, Carla."

Carla settled herself into the stool, allowing her chin to rest under her propped hand. "I see therapy is *really* helping."

"It sure *is*." I returned the sarcasm, perhaps a bit too much. "I'm certainly recovering well after seeing five of my classmates die right in front of my eyes. Maybe I deserve a gold star. What do you think?"
"I didn't mean it like that, Sam." Carla said, those fierce hazel eyes shooting me with exasperation. "It's just... You've been in therapy for over a year now and Mrs. Pierre said you'd start to... you know, take the proper steps to heal."

I scoffed—this is why I loathed therapists, psychiatrists, or any other person who declared that their knowledge had superiority over my feelings. Damn Mrs. Pierre, with her hideous dresses and her sunny disposition. Who was she to determine the next steps of my life, let alone fill my parents and best friends with empty promises? Absolutely absurd, if you ask me.

"I'm trying"

"Are you?" She looked at me, concern brimming underneath the frustration.

"You've been so different since that day and-"

"I watched five people die right in front of me, Carla. One by one, shot. Stripped from this Earth. Blood everywhere. Screams and sobs, pleads for mercy,"

"I didn't mean it that way Sam."

"No, maybe you are denying it to yourself, but you like all others feel that I should be taken to the psych ward. Millions of people have already given me enough charity. I don't need or want more, especially if it's something that you feel obligated to do. You don't need to stick around if you can't handle my emotions."

Carla's eyes softened momentarily and her lips parted. "What are you saying, exactly?"

I closed my eyes.

(Easy, Samantha

Easy,

Nice and easy)

"I'm saying that you don't need to feel compelled to stay."

Carla's lips trembled. "Is that what you seriously think of me?" Her voice cracked softly. She crossed her arms, a look of betrayal painting her face. "Do you seriously think that I feel forced to stay in this, Samantha?"

I looked away, like a coward—the coward I am, perhaps. My eyes focused on a small stain that decorated the usually pristine white tiles. "Your actions would defend that." I uttered.

She responded with a scoff. "You're kidding me, right?"

My forehead began to boil with perspiration, so I remained silent and began to count backwards—a small gesture to reduce anxiety, according to Mrs. Pierre. The one thing she said that actually became useful in my wretched life.

(5, the sweat
4, the footsteps
3, the murmurs

2, the announcement
"YOU'RE ALL GOING TO DIE!"
1, BOOM!)

"So, what does this mean?"

I didn't want to look up, but I also didn't want to look any more helpless than I already did.

Slowly, I brought my eyes to Carla again, sighing softly. "It means whatever you want it to mean."

Carla's jaw tightened and she huffed, exasperation once again radiating from her hazel eyes.

Then, she spoke.

"You're breaking this years old friendship with me, aren't you?"

I sighed, biting my lower lip. I didn't know, truthfully—was this the breaking point of our 14-year-friendship? Possibly. I didn't know, like how I don't know most things anymore.

My delay in response irritated Carla and she
got up, shaking her head. "I don't want to
deal with this anymore," Her hand rose,
gesturing to me in a hostile manner. I
flinched, but she didn't seem to regard these
signals of distress. As a matter of fact, she
continued, raising her voice now. "You
seriously need help, Samantha." She hissed,
stomping over to the counter and retrieving
her handbag. Then, she aggressively threw
it over her shoulder, before shooting me one
final look of raw betrayal. "Don't
bother calling me anymore, got it?"

I didn't say anything, I just blinked—lost, as
the door slammed and Carla went along
with the cool wind and grey sky of Seattle.

Five years have passed since that day, and I
never saw her again. Mrs. Pierre offered me
a bunch of pity after I informed her
about everything, but I didn't have the
mental capacity to entertain it. I seriously
couldn't bring myself to. Carla left, that was
her choice. I've made mine now; it is time I
move on too.

Move on from everything, I mean.
Move on from the day my innocence was
tarnished.

Move on from the loss, the anguish.
Move on from the screams.
Move on from the little creatures who visit
me in my dreams.
Move on from Carla, who was my sanity and
talisman.

I don't know where this path will take me,
or what void I'll fall into next.

Clearly God has a peculiar journey intended
for me, based on the experiences I've
endured already.
Who knows,
Who knows.
But, I suppose I'll find out eventually.

Goodbye, Dark Days.
Samantha Monroe

Lessons I Learnt From The Gita

I don't know much of Sanskrit but after hearing so many stories from the Bhagavad Gita from my mother I was curious about what was so special about it. So, I decided that I would read Bhagavad Gita in English from the Internet, and, although it is not the same as reading the original Gita, it would give me some perspective into what it all was about.

I learned that Bhagavad Gita is meant for those who wish to transcend all confusion. When you are confused in your search for truth, then the removal of that kind of confusion will bring enlightenment to one and all.

Bhagavad Gita has been endearing to all those who seek Truth, who look for perfection, who are interested in a complete science of everything, irrespective of caste, creed, religion, and nationality. This holy book presents the science of life, as it is, which was originally spoken to Arjun by Lord Krishna, the Supreme Personality of Godhead in the battlefie of Mahabharata approximately 5000 years ago.

What The Bhagavad Gita Taught Me?

It taught me to think of the main and deeper questions rather than the questions, we are condition to ask.

Such as, "Who am I?", "What is my relation with Supreme?" rather than "What is the new web series?" or "What will I do after 5 years?"

It taught me the importance of human life. It taught me how this human life is rare and God has already made every arrangement for survival.

For example, when a child is born, instantly the mother's milk is within reach to feed the child but we have created artificial necessities in life and we waste our lives chasing these artificial necessities.
I got to know that there is so much identity crisis in the world that people don't know the purpose of life. Rather than finding it they are just busy enjoying superficial things

Our real identity is that we are spirit souls and we are, by nature, always happy (Sat chit ananda) – that's why we chase happiness everywhere but we are always trying to find happiness in matters which are dead or in temporary things like family, country, etc., but our attempts are not successful because we never get continuous happiness, whereas, our nature is eternal and we want everlasting happiness.

We are in a prison house and this world is so uncertain that anything could happen at any moment with us, so we have to prepare from now itself – How to detach my mind from temporary things and attach it to Krishna to pursue our real goal to get back our eternal svarupa in the spiritual world?

If I can practice how to love God, then only I can love everyone selflessly and selfless love is the real happiness – you can see practically how a mother although eats nothing but is happy to feed her child. If you can similarly love God then that is the perfection of life

We have to start situating ourself in neutral platform and seeing things without being biased as Hindu or Muslim , rich or poor, boy or girl, etc., because these are all ephemeral designations of the body.

How Bhagavad Gita helped me?

I waste less time now as I have at least realized this that this human body is not for just enjoying but to find out about me and my relationship with the world and the real happiness is that which comes directly from the soul, not from external objects.

As a partially changed human, I will ask all those in search of true happiness to read the Bhagavad Gita as it will change your life too, and if not, it will atleat teach you lessons which will help you climb the stairs to success!

Every Night, I Counted The Stars.....

Every night, I counted the stars, towards freedom, waiting for this emptiness beside me to flee away. Each day, each night and each moment indeed felt like a huge weight of existential dread. The Covid 19 pandemic had turned my life into an unfinished thought – well-intentioned in the beginning but falling flat during execution. We didn't get to sustain such thoughts to be left unfinished. Writing this confined between four walls. Stuck at home. I'm able to see no more than a few people on the road and a piece of blue winter sky squeezed between the buildings through my window. But this window has been like a breath to me in the last months – my only connection to nature and to the external world. I go there every half hour just to watch the time go by and the magic of changing light.

Sitting like a trapped bird in my room, I'm remembering all the amazing experiences I've had in my life in the last few years. But I also remember the countless days or months I've lost on, with superficial concerns and unfounded worries. Or, worst of all, how many great experiences I've missed just out of fear or laziness. Things have changed, and it's a bit scary to imagine how the world we'll now face will be different from the world we knew so far. Every second we spend angry, bored in front of a digital screen, or lost in something we don't really want to be doing, is a second less to follow our dreams, to have new experiences, to stay with whom we wish to stay.

May we learn from our past mistakes and this hard moment lead us to a more conscious state.

Knitting Threads Of Loneliness

The old woman sat there, silently clutching the scuffed knitting needles in her worn, leathery hands. They clinked together rhythmically as she continued working on the scarf that no one would end up wearing. She stared with beady bloodshot eyes into the distance, there was no need to observe her hands, they did as they pleased. The old oak rocking chair with the plush floral-patterned cushion creaked as the aged wood stretched back and forth. The faint breeze swayed the red plastic hummingbird feeder to her right, the sun's rays bouncing off it and illuminating the crimson material. The wind reverberated off the metal of the dangling windchimes by the paint-peeling front door. A soft symphonic sound. The breeze brought the gentle scent of sweet wildflowers and cedar trees. The beautiful weather and refreshing smells almost fought back against the perpetual feeling of loneliness and despair.

Note From The Author

My Dear Readers,

Thank You for appreciating my work and supporting me by reading this book. If you want to comment on the book, please mail me at swaranyagupta.2007@gmail.com. I will definitely mail you back whenever I
have the time to do so!

Now, let us end this book with a poem because I can't wait to share it with you!

Help Me

Help Me,

I'm barely breathing,
Drowning in the waves of my tears,
Laying down in my defeat.

As I'm dying, hiding, lying, and sighing,
"Help Me!", I yell,
Trying to find someone to tell,
But as water submerges my lungs,
The cold water leaves my senses stung,
As I grow numb.

Before I pass out,
I think if there is and ever was,
A saviour to pull me out of the devil's jaws,
But I know that there never was and never
will,
Only I can pull myself up.

And with all my strength,
I run to my hill,
So when the sun shines,
And where I can perhaps resign,
From life and from pain.

As I mount my silver haired mare,

Her flowing tail and mane,
Blowing in the wind,
As I ride off into the sunset,
All my pain and anger would at last leave,
All my sadness and hate would at last subdue,
As my mind would finally be put at ease.

About The Author

Swaranya Gupta is a 15-year-old school student studying in Delhi Public School Ruby Park, Kolkata, India. Her hobbies and interests mainly include writing poetry and stories, quizzing, drawing and singing. She is also an avid reader. Her interest in reading has helped her hone her creative writing and communication skills. She prefers writing poetry which has an arching theme of sadness and sorrow. She finds poetry as a medium of communication and comfort between people as well as a coping mechanism and hopes to give her readers the same comfort. Her mother is her biggest inspiration. For the future, she has big dreams and goals, and, she aspires to reach to the finish line with good intentions in her mind and love for family and friends in her heart.

The End

62

www.ingramcontent.com/pod-product-compliance
Lightning Source LLC
Chambersburg PA
CBHW021325160726

47994CB00004B/1609